SAVANNAH

FT. FREDERICA
FT. ST. SIMONS

FT. ST. ANDREWS
FT. WILLIAM

ST. AUGUSTINE

FT. ST. SIMONS

JEKYLL IS.

E

N   S

W   Critt Graham

THE
BLOODY SUMMER
OF 1742
A Colonial Boy's Journal

Written by Joyce Blackburn
Illustrated by Critt Graham

For Joseph, remembering
when we went to Fort Frederica
together & hoping we'll do it
again in 2001. Hug!
Joyce

John Campbell MacLeod lived only in the imagination of the author. However, the events recorded by him are mostly true to the historical records. This "journal" is intended to help us remember the place, Fort Frederica, and its importance in the colony of Georgia.

The following note and the journal to which it refers were found upon the death of Widow Flora MacLeod four years later among her few possessions. Whether or not her son returned to Darien in the colony of Georgia is not known.

Fort Frederica
St. Simons Island
7 June 1742

Honoured Mamma, since coming down river from Darien with Capt. Mackay, he has arranged for me to stay here with the Thomas Walkers. I can work for my keep. Thank you for the Blank Book. I will try to write in it every day. Maybe that will improve my hand and my spelling.

Your devoted son,
John Campbell MacLeod

The first entry in John's journal was dated 10 June 1742.

10 June 1742

At sunrise, I waked scared out of my wits by a sound at the window - a brushing sound - on the glass. I lay still and listened. Then I heard a shrill *wheeeeep*. It was a flycatcher snatching spider eggs. He even waked the roosters!

My room is five feet by five feet and eight inches. The window faces east. I can look down and see the sentry and hear him call Who Goes? before he opens the gate. Being upstairs, I can see on the other side of the ten foot high cedar wall. A wide walk of planks spans the moat there. When the Regiment comes in from an expedition, the clatter and rumble is like thunder - echoing back and forth from the east pasture to the river beyond the opposite gate - the Fort gate.

The Walkers will let me stay the summer. In the room next to mine is Lt. Sterling and his soldier-servant. Thomas Walker and wife and two children sleep downstairs. Every morning, when I smell biscuits baking, I dress and run to the privy. There is a tub of water on the back stoop. I splash my face. Today, the water was warm. It did not cool in the night, because the sun is now hot enough by noon to blister.

Mr. Walker was already waiting for me in the kitchen. He motioned for me to sit at his left. He made the stools and table board of yellow pine and showed me how to hollow out a trencher and noggin for my own.

Mrs. Walker makes tasty porridge and gives me plenty. But I could *live* on her corn biscuits. She bakes twice a day. The Publick Bakery near the barracks will not get her trade! There is always honey for the biscuits. Mr. Walker keeps bees.

"Bein' King's Carpenter leaves little time for anything besides," he told me. "But bees are understandin'...they know I will not neglect them on purpose."

"I heard a lot of bees in that old hollow oak where the path goes into the South Woods," I said.

"Ah yes, gall berry bushes a plenty in them woods. Bee bread." Without giving me time to ask what that was, Mr. Walker said, "Don't stuff your cheeks with biscuit, Little Jack."

How did he know my mouth was too full, he was not looking at me? He is strict. He has an old book, *Youth's Behavior*, from which he reads aloud such as, "Sup not broth at table, but eat it with a spoon." Then he looks at *me*. He should read it to the Regiment!

Why does he call me Little Jack? I am four feet, ten inches.

11 June 1742

Today, I will help Mr. Walker select beams for the Guard House. He is teaching me how to slice out knots in the logs with an axe.

"See here, Little Jack, this knot is a no good one," he says. "A vertical is a no good knot."

I ask, "Can one knot make a difference?"

"This one would weaken a beam, and beams are bones, the bones of a roof. Here on this island, they must be strong against the winds."

His hands are hard but he touches the wood in a friendly sort of way.

Before we start work in the shop for the day, there is a drill of the regulars and some citizens. Like at Darien, every house has its musket, bayonet, flint, and powder. I watch on the Parade and will learn the arms exercise.

Order your firelock
Rest your firelock
Poise your firelock

That is how the Sergeant always begins. When I have the rest of the orders memorized, I will ask for a musket of my own. I may need it. I overheard Captain Carr, coxswain of the Frederica scout boat, say that the Governor of Cuba, under orders of King Philip V of Spain, is sending a big expedition up the coast.

If we cannot turn them back, they will burn every military post and settlement between here and Port Royal in the Carolina Colony. That must be why General Oglethorpe is here on St. Simons most of the time these days. This Island may have to be defended.

12 June 1742

Three thunder storms followed after my entry yesterday. The first shower doused the military drill. When the companies "cast about to charge" - step eleven in the arms exercise - water splashed around their ankles. The rain came down so hard and of a sudden, I could barely see. That is why today the myrtle trees and hedges at the Barracks are sprouting uniforms and boots. The soldiers hang them out to dry. No wonder they complain of this season. Most have only one change of clothes, so keeping dry is not easy. Even the officers swear at the wet. Major Harrison said,

11

"The mildew will bury us before the Spanish get here. Mildew 'n rust 'n muskettos 'n vermin!" His oaths I dare not record.

Earlier this evening, Mrs. Walker had me burn some tarry rags to drive away the clouds of insects. But with the dark falling now, I feel them. The sand flies pester my ears, my eyes and mouth. I have two candles. I will light them both.

From the marshes, frogs and alligators bark. Next door, at Ann Bennett's Tavern, I can hear the Regiment's drunken singing. I guess they are trying to forget the heat and bad weather and their fear that the Spanish may attack us.

Now I hear a commotion on the dock off from the southwest bastion of the Fort. Could be Indians and Rangers arriving with intelligence reports for General Oglethorpe. All the singing and whoops have 'roused the neighbors' geese! It is not often quiet here - only in the deep woods or down a ways on the river.

13 June 1742

Between the buzzing of the flies and muskettos in my very ears and the hollers of soldiers and Indians barbequing a pig they had stolen, last night was one devilish dream for me. There are mean red welts all over my bod. They make me feverish. My eyes and even my head feel swolled!

"The Heats are bad enough without these Itches," Mrs. Walker said. She bathed my bites with vinegar. "You best stay in the house." Which I did until she sent me to the garden for pease and squash.

At noon we had a real feast. The Indian Toonahowi brought oysters and a great Flat fish. Mrs. Walker made a stuffing of corn meal with the Oysters and baked the fish. The vegetables and a melon made a welcome change from every day pork and rice. There are no left-overs for supper. Mr. Walker and Toonahowi toasted the King with strong beer. We ate from good pewter plates. This Toonahowi is an important person.

Very little stirs for a couple of hours after this main meal. It is too hot and sultry.

Last night, during all the carousing noise and rain, a tall, tall pine was striken by lightning. The Indians say that is a sign of War. Mr. Walker says they are "dumb superstitious." Just the same, when I sneeze he says, "God bless you!" If it happens to be Monday, he says, "Sneeze on Monday, sneeze for danger. Sneeze on Tuesday, kiss a stranger." He thinks sneezes are omens. Lightning is not.

He got two of the soldiers to help him take down the tree. He will make good use of it.

By late afternoon I was searching for something to do when John Hird, the Constable's son who lives right behind us, came to the fence and yelled, "Let's go for a swim!" There is a good deep hole 'round the curve below the Fort. From there, you can see why the General picked this place. The spur in front of the King's Magazine projects into the Frederica River. There is a clear line of fire in both directions, but you have to come almost the whole way 'round the curve to spot it.

The cannon are mounted on a platform some ten feet above the high tide mark behind a sod wall. The sods have been placed on the slope like bricks.

We would like to slide down the bank, but we cannot even get inside the Fort palisades. From where we swim, close to shore, you see only trees. The Spanish would never guess a fort was just 'round the bend. General Oglethorpe means for it to be a surprise, of course, unlike Fort St. Simons on the south end of the Island visible from the Sound. The watch-tower there keeps a lookout for every ship coming in. As soon as one is sighted, signal guns are fired. If it looks suspicious, a horseman is dispatched to Oglethorpe's Frederica headquarters.

Four years ago, he had a road built to connect the two forts.

14 June 1742

The best thing about yesterday afternoon was that I was excused from work. When we got to the river Toonahowi and his scouts were swimming and diving with other boys from the village. He is a great favorite of General Oglethorpe. You remember when the General took his best friend, Chief Tomochichi, to England to prove to the King how loyal the Creek Indians were to the Crown? Toonahowi, who was a boy then, went along and was given a gold pocket watch by the Duke of Cumberland. He still carries it. He speaks and writes educated English, and he is said to be the General's most trusted scout. Toonahowi's Indian spies range down the coast from here to St. Augustine and all the way up to Augusta and over the mainland to the west.

"The Spanish *and* French cannot so much as breathe in secret," Toonahowi laughs. "We know all." He boasts like all great warriors.

He pointed across the river as an alligator slid off the mud bank and started toward us. We all swam in to shore behind Toonahowi and scrambled out of the water.

"Your knees are knobby, Little Jack," he said. No doubt he will tease me when I wear my Highland kilt, too.

John Hird pulled on his britches and shirt without drying off, because his father whistled for him. That sound carries from one end of town to the other. The Constable whistles with his mouth, but we cannot figure how no matter how much we try to imitate him. If we succeeded, he might not like it. He takes his duties of keeping order very seriously.

I later learned that he called John to help drive some hogs and sheep back to the pasture outside the town gate, but they had already trampled the moat embankment. Constable Hird then put a notice on Ann Bennett's Tavern door that the owners would be taken before the Magistrate. And whoever let his cow stray right down Broad Street helping herself to the tender new leaves of the bordering orange and peach trees will be found out.

The townsmen will probably ignore the summons. They have a saying, "Preacher Hird squawks like a bird." They think he has his hands full protecting us from robbery and rape and even murder. His is not a popular job. Some claim Hird is overly pious. He used to be a Quaker back in England. But coming over to the Colony, John Wesley converted him. He even wears a wig now like Wesley. He observes the Wesley disciplines and conducts morning prayers in his home. He keeps records of who attends. If that is how he tells sinners from saints, Frederica is far from religious.

At table, I have heard Mr. Walker talk about when Charles Wesley took his leave of Georgia six years ago. He was accused of being a gossip, a trouble-maker, and the General was relieved to be rid of him. And the Reverend John Wesley's very life was threatened in this town. He openly said he despaired of doing any good here. The next minister, William Norris, was accused of fornication. And the last military chaplain, Edward Dyson, died of drink.

It is not surprising that Constable Thomas Hird, lay minister, thinks he has a divine mission in this isolated military post. But his flock is small, indeed.

Last Sunday he moved the congregation out under the trees near the town gate. I listened to him read the high phrases and wished for my own copy of *The Book of Common Prayer.*

"The Scripture moveth us, in sundry places, to acknowledge and confess our manifold sins and wickedness...."

Without telling Constable Hird, I directly asked God to forgive me for tying Mrs. Walker's two laying hens together so they would fight and raise a ruckus.

We sang from the Scottish Psalter. I like to sing. My voice does not sound like mine though. It is neither high nor low. It startles me and is raspy as a hickory hinge.

15 June 1742

Probably the page about Constable Hird should best be torn out and burned. He is not a bad man - just severe. He lets son John climb trees with me and swing on grapevines in the woods. And his daughter Phoebe likes me. That is because I show her how to spin my top on the palm of her hand. She says it tickles. Then I tickle *her*. Phoebe can produce two skeins of linen thread in a day just like her mother. Enough of Phoebe! But she *is* pretty.

Toonahowi asked Mr. Walker if he could "borrow" me today. I am to meet him at the blacksmith's after the companies drill on the Parade. I am very excited! How can I wait!

Later the Same Day

It is now evening. The insects swirl around the flame of my candle and make waves of noise outside. So much has happened. I feel as though I dreamed it, but I will try to remember.

Toonahowi is taller up close than he looks from a distance. He is brown and lean and limber - limber as a sassafras sapling. He is strong. When he shook hands, his grip told me he could easily lift me off my feet and throw me over his shoulder. Everyone in the Colony knows that he is the great-nephew and adopted son of Tomochichi. Since the great Tomochichi's death three years ago, General Oglethorpe, who loved the Chief like a brother, has given Toonahowi more and more authority. He and his runner-spies come here to report in person to the General what the Spanish are up to. The French, too, over west.

I have heard the men of the Regiment tell how brave he was when he led a bunch of Creek Indians on Oglethorpe's expedition against St. Augustine. It was a bitter defeat, but Toonahowi captured a Spanish officer who turned out to be Don Romualdo Ruiz. His uncle had been governor of Florida. Upon delivering him to Oglethorpe, the story-tellers claim Toonahowi said, "Big Fish!"

For two months after that, the General was sick with fever. Toonahowi still brings him camphor bags to wear around his neck.

Capt. Mackay told Toonahowi that I am good with horses. That is why I was "borrowed" to help take six horses to the south end of the island, to Fort St. Simons which I had never seen. The horses are probably needed to patrol the beach down there. Blacksmith Harding had shoed them. As usual, a few children and town loafers were watching the fireworks of the forge - blasts of white sparks forced by the bellows from the fire up the chimney. The sounds are as agreeable as the sight - the roaring, creaking, thumping, tapping have tones and rhythm.

Toonahowi actually spit on his thumb and forefinger and picked up a live coal to light his pipe. Fine ash from the green chestnut wood kept all of us batting our eyes. I choked on the smoke. But there is something wondrous about the way iron turns brighter and brighter red. Then white. Blacksmith Harding knows just when to pull it out of the fire or douse it in the slack tub or put it on the anvil. He can flatten it with his big hammer. Like a bell, the strokes clang.

I could have watched longer, but Toonahowi motioned, Follow. "Not so fast there, Little Jack," the blacksmith yelled. "You can shovel up those horse droppings before you take the beasts away." I did as I was ordered. The droppings smelled gassy in the hot sun. There is a thick haze from the heavy dews and heat.

A lot of whispering goes up and down Broad Street about Blacksmith Harding living with Widow May Spencer, in *her* house. They are not married yet. A soldier said, "There will never be enough women to go around in this god-forsaken place. Harding is a lucky one."

Toonahowi never seems in a hurry. Once outside the town gate, past some neglected weedy garden plots and onto the Military Road, he let the horses graze in the big meadow while he showed me the tiny little star inside the fruit of a prickly pear cactus. We even tasted it - mealy, with a hint of sweet. He divided some dried venison he carries in a deerskin pouch. I wonder what else he has in it.

We collected the horses and passed through a thin stand of pines and gums onto a savannah which I knew provided good hay for our animals. But it was my first time to go beyond the common pasture outside the Frederica gate, so I was not prepared for the surprise of General Oglethorpe's simple two-story board and tabby cottage which we could view up a shaded lane. Between the lane and the road where we were, was a garden, grape arbor, and orchard. I saw *acres* of orange, mulberry and fig trees. Here there are no weeds. It is said weeds bring out the General's temper.

Toonahowi pointed at a family of raccoon feasting up in a fig tree nearby. They acted tame and looked at us curiously through their little black masks. The robbers!

"The General has many pets from the wild," Toonahowi said. "They are not Spaniards." He laughed.

When we reached Gully Hole Creek where the lane from the General's place merged with the Military Road, Toonahowi pulled some stems of marsh grass and had me taste the white root ends. They were salty. Then he cut out a palmetto heart and sliced off the bottom of it.

"Here, try this," he said. The flavor made me think of wild asparagus. He knows every root, berry, leaf, mushroom - which is safe to eat, which is poison.

He pokes fun at our "British appetites for costly provisions". I got to figuring. Mrs. Hawkins sells milk for 4 pence a quart. Chickens cost 4 pence. The soldiers pay 14 pence a quart for Madeira wine. The Indians get 9 pence a bushel for their corn.

Gen. Oglethorpe's Farm

"One order of medicines from London costs Dr. Hawkins over 29 pence," Toonahowi said with scorn. "We make our own. I must admit my weakness for your garden pease and beans and herbs and fancy fruits." His black eyes danced and glistened.

For the next five miles, he talked about General Oglethorpe. About being taken with Tomochichi's party to London eight years ago. His Majesty King George II sent for the Indians to be driven to Court in his own coaches! They met Queen Caroline, the Archbishop, the Duke of Cumberland, all kinds of royalty, the Trustees, everyone!

He talked, too, about how close his uncle Chief Tomochichi had been to the General from their very first meeting at Yamacraw.

"I am the fortunate heir of that friendship." There was love in Toonahowi's voice. "My uncle always called the General The Great Man. So he is. I shall not forget his grief when my uncle died. He helped carry the coffin to the burial in the central square in Savannah while a bell tolled and muffled drums beat. The Great Man wept. He wept with my people. I shall not forget."

"Now you are here to help him, aren't you?" I asked.

"Yes, you can smell Danger in the air. My scouts tell me that near-hurricane winds and rain are holding the Spanish in St. Augustine. Once the weather breaks, they will come."

He stopped one of the horses and leaped on its back.

"Let me lift you up, Little Jack. We will ride the rest of the way."

We rode out of a thicket onto a causeway built of logs. It crossed a marshy area. We led the horses single file, because it was narrow, and they were skittish, especially when they heard a platoon of Highlanders coming toward us. Such a racket! The Sergeant called, "March!" A bagpipe screeched, a drum beat rat-a-tat-tat. Toonahowi saluted the colors. So did I.

By now you cannot read my writing because my eyes are about to close. I am tired and the muskettos are carrying bits of me away. What I learned at Fort St. Simons must wait until tomorrow. What a day Toonahowi and I have had!

16 June 1742,

Yesterday, when we came out of the marshy place and through a tangle of wax myrtle and grape vines, it was like passing from a pitch-dark room into a huge one lit with a thousand candles. The beach on the southern tip of this island is much wider than I had expected. Stretching beyond it is the sea and sky...on and on...I gulped the air and wished I were one of the gulls high in the sunlight.

Even before Toonahowi pointed it out, I spotted the watchtower and the stockade at Fort St. Simons. A little farther on - on the very southeastern tip of land - there was a whitewashed blockhouse. When we got closer, there were lots of huts and gardens where the soldiers live with their cattle and goats.

"That white tabby building with the horseshoe shaped embankment is Delegal's Fort." Toonahowi gestured toward the blockhouse some four hundred yards away. We dismounted and walked to it.

"Those three cannon are 18-pounders. They guard the harbor," he said. "And over there to the west at Fort St. Simons are seven more cannon. Look in between." There were five more.

Hauling ammunition and supplies into nearby magazines, soldiers scurried around like fiddler crabs. A Corporal with a big grin shouted, "Toonahowi!" He had been watching for us to bring the horses. You could tell he looked up to my Indian friend. They turned from me and talked in low voices. I heard only snatches..."better defenses"..."invasion"...enough to set me wondering. When? When would the Spanish attack? Where? Here on the south end or up at Frederica? I wished I had me a bar-

21

rel of those grenades they were stacking inside Fort St. Simons!

The area between the two forts is level and high - high enough to see past the beach and down the Sound any ships coming into harbor. The next island to the south, Jekyll, seemed within hailing distance. The tide was out, and I think I could have waded across, but Toonahowi says the channel is deeper than it looks. He says that shallow bottomed ships can easily pass to Gascoigne's plantation on the western bluff.

We counted one hundred and twenty soldiers' huts. The Corporal estimated three hundred of our men would be assembled by the end of the month. General Oglethorpe hoped for many more, Toonahowi said, especially from Carolina.

Behind the two forts, a rim of live oaks sheltered a few homes of Island settlers. Their goats nibbled nearby. What a peaceful picture that made. Then when I turned around and faced the Sound again, there were the guns and cannon, the companies drilling, practicing to obey commands.

Prime and load
Shoulder your firelock
Make ready
Present
Fire

The volleys of musket fire boomed out over the water and smoke billowed up hiding the sun.

Just then the Corporal returned from the stables leading a high-stepping shiny black horse. My heart beat loud as the drums when he handed me the reins.

"The General's horse, Little Jack," Toonahowi smiled.

"He went off on the sloop *Faulcon* to Fort St. Andrews down on Cumberland Island," the Corporal explained. "He may have taken along Horton who commands the grenadier company over there on Jekyll. Once the Spanish fleet is sighted from Cumberland, word will be brought here."

The Corporal patted the black horse, adjusted the saddle and stirrups. "He will sail back to Frederica this afternoon, and you can have the horse waiting for him at the dock." The Corporal kept saying *he* with great respect.

Toonahowi handed me up. "The saddle is for you, Little Jack. I am not accustomed to English leather." He laughed, leaping up behind me. The Corporal gave the horse a little slap on the thigh and away we went.

The ride back to Frederica was the fastest I have ever had. When a thunderstorm overtook us, that horse raced right out from under it, and we were waiting when the *Faulcon* docked at the Fort.

"Here comes the General!" Toonahowi grabbed my hand and pulled me toward a man surrounded by officers and Indian scouts.

The man saw us. "Toonahowi! You brought my horse from the south end." He strode up to us and embraced my Indian friend.

"Yes, I did, Sir, with the help of John Campbell MacLeod here."

The General who was tall and thin leaned down and shook my hand. All I had voice to say was, "How do you do, Sir."

"You are the boy from Darien, the one Mackay brought down...the one he calls Little Jack. Am I right?" His gray eyes looked right through me, but they were friendly.

"Yes, Sir," I said.

"Bring him with you, Toonahowi, when you come to my house." Quickly he mounted the black horse and rode toward the town gate at a gallop. Toonahowi claims my mouth was still open with amazement when we reached home. Mr. Walker agreed. They both teased me and said I might be too excited to sleep.

24

17 June 1742

Two nights have passed since I began writing about my trip to the south end. I can report that Mr. Walker's prediction was dead wrong. My sleep has been sound even if my dreams were full of Indians and horses.

Yesterday was anything but exciting. It rained so hard the moat almost filled up. Mrs. Walker had saved up a lot of chores for me to do. For one thing, she sent me to Calwell's for candles. On the way up Broad a cart and wagon passed me. The drivers were racing right through the puddles. I was as speckled as a clapper rail's eggs.

Calwell greeted me with a disapproving look. My boots squished and left tracks of water and mud on his floor. He is known to be particular and a bit heady with importance since the General himself taught him surveying and encouraged him to engage in trade and shipping. Calwell's sloop has a mooring at the fort dock. A Tallow Chandler is prosperous no matter how hard the times!

That must be why he is Third Magistrate here - it's his success. His son brags that Charles Wesley baptized him by "true immersion." Hear, Hear! I suspect Calwell had the plans for his new house unrolled on the counter of his shop so that all customers would notice. At a glance, I saw that it was to have three stories with shutters at every window, even on the out buildings. "It will be the finest place in this town for trade," he remarked. I do admit that Calwell is a man of many talents and "endowments of the mind" to quote Mr. Walker.

Calwell tied the candles in two bundles. "Better slip these inside your shirt, Little Jack," he said. "A wet wick makes a poor light." I did as he said. "And tell the Walkers the water is rising in the fort moat."

Just as I stepped outside the chandler's shop, the heavens emptied. This rain could flood the town I thought. Already drenched, I wrested off my boots, crammed the bundles into them, then tucked a boot under each arm and waded on to the Fort. I knew of a crack between two warped palisade posts through which I often looked. Sure enough, the high winds and tide and downpours had pushed the water to the brim of the moat banks. If the Spanish were to come now, I thought, we could drown the lot of them and never fire a shot!

By the time I got home with the candles, the rain had stopped, the sun was bright, the sky blue again. The birds were as happy as I was. Only Mrs. Walker was not happy.

"These candles are as soaked as your English boots. A wet wick..."

"Makes a poor light," I finished for her. "I am sorry, Mrs. Walker."

"Sorry can not cure distemper," she snapped. "Take your bod to bed and leave your wet things on the stair landing. I'll dry them out. You'll be growin' moss between your toes! This island climate! 'Tis true as the saying goes, 'In the spring a paradise, in the summer a hell, and in the autumn a hospital!'"

That was my punishment, staying naked in bed the rest of this irksome, tedious day. But Mrs. Walker did bring me a cup of hot coffee with milk. A treat usually forbidden us children. With the coffee was one of her raisin tarts.

When Mr. Walker came in from his woodworking shed at dark, he brought up my dried clothes. "These boots are as stiff as Governor Bull's neck," he growled.

Everyone here is furious with the Carolina Governor's refusal to send down reinforcements.

"I have a message for you, Little Jack, from Toonahowi." I held my breath until Mr. Walker said, "He asked me if you could go with him over to the General's place." He turned to walk out the door. "I told him you could if it does not rain tomorrow."

"Tomorrow?" my voice barely squeaked.

26

Mr. Walker did not answer but clumped on down the stair. I will go to sleep without telling him about the high water. Tomorrow, it will have drained back into the river. Everything will be as usual, except for me. For me, tomorrow holds another expedition with my Indian friend!

Please, please, Almighty God, I beseech Thee, restrain these immoderate rains wherewith Thou hast afflicted us. Please let tomorrow dawn fair that I may give thanks unto Thy name, through Jesus Christ our Lord. Amen.

18 June 1742

God heard my plea. He granted a cloudless day. I dressed in my best homespun blouse, though I did not fancy its ruffled stock and full sleeves, nor would I agree to wear my kilt even when Mrs. Walker insisted.

"You do not want to be presentable on your first visit to General Oglethorpe?" Her eyebrows arched in dismay!

"This is not a rejoicing day, Mrs. Walker," I said. "I may be grooming The Great Man's horse. My boots and blue linen britches will best serve that occupation."

You could hear Mrs. Walker's sigh all the way to Darien. "You are right, of course," she said, but she looked so rejected, I quickly hugged her. She blushed with surprise.

I ran to join Toonahowi waiting on the stoop. By then the sun cast sharp flat shadows on the road to the General's place which is known to all of us here as The Farm.

"I'll race you up the lane," Toonahowi said. And so, in spite of the shade, we arrived at the General's front door sweating and breathless. The trust servant who answered our knock looked at us disapprovingly but ushered us into a cool, simply furnished room where the General was dictating to his secretary, Mr. Francis Moore. Besides the table and chairs where they worked, there was a settee and other chairs, an enormous desk piled with magazines and maps and documents, stacks of leather bound books. A large engraving of His Majesty, King George II, hung over the fireplace, a watercolor painting of Loch Arkaig on one wall, a gilt-framed mirror on another. I could not help overhearing that the General was writing to Captain Hardy of the Carolina navy. Ships and supplies were needed immediately.

Mr. Moore finished the letter with a flourish of his quill and handed it to the General who read and signed it. The secretary sprinkled sand on the large signature to blot the ink, and the General stood up.

"Mr. Moore, if Governor Bull ignores this the way he did my personal messengers, Primrose Maxwell and Hugh Mackay, I may have to send *you* to Carolina. You could convince him!"

The General strode toward us, smiling. "Toonahowi! Little Jack! What a welcome relief from the Petulant Behavior of Governors and their Parasites!"

He was over six feet tall, straight like an arrow but easy in his movements. His face was tanned and weather-beaten. I felt comfortable at once. Maybe it was because he wore a velvet cap instead of a wig, and because he talked so much. He and my Indian friend laughed a lot even though they discussed latest Intelligence. When Toonahowi told him that the Spanish fleet was about to sail north, General Oglethorpe's big round eyes blazed.

"Let them come," he said firmly. Suddenly his face was alert, his hand gripped the ornamented hilt of his sword. "We are preparing. We will not be taken by surprise."

He turned away toward the open window and his whole body relaxed. "Smell the sweet william and pepperbush, Little Jack." He inhaled deeply, wrinkling his beak of a nose. "I will have my overseer, Manly, order a bouquet for you to take to Mrs. Walker, along with a basket of plums." Then he looked at me directly. "Toonahowi tells me you are much attached to that horse Colonel Cecil gave me. Is that so?"

I said, "Yes, Sir. That is so."

"And the horse likes you." He put his hand on my shoulder. "How would you like to help care for him until the Emergency is passed? I want to be sure he is ready for me at any moment."

"I would consider it an honor, Sir."

He shook hands as though I were grown up. "That's settled then. Show Little Jack the stables, Toonahowi, and we will talk later."

The rest of the afternoon, I spent learning how best to groom and feed and exercise that handsome animal. We have a secret way of understanding each other, already.

Toonahowi stayed with the General. But at supper time, I ran most of the way to town. The sentry at the town gate gave me a curious look.

"Where did you get the flowers and plums, young'un? Steal 'em?"

"None of your affair," I sassed. He opened the gate. I felt bold and reckless. I made up a song as I raced home, "I have been to The Farm, The Farm, The Farm...."

19 June 1742

Mr. Walker found out about the horse last night after Mrs. Walker chattered on and on, "Can you believe Little Jack was invited to The Farm"...On and on and on. Mr. Walker did not say so, but I could sense his disapproval. He kept leafing through his *Almanak* without a word. Usually, he reads aloud.

This morning I rose early to go over to the General's stables in order to get back here for breakfast. That was when Mr. Walker reminded me that he is boarding me in exchange for helping *him*. "There is quite enough industry here, Little Jack, for both of us. The General has trust servants a plenty to tend his animals."

"It is only one horse, Mr. Walker," I said. "He needs me."

"Horses do not need men, Little Jack. Men need horses."

"Must I tell General Oglethorpe?"

"Tell him what, Little Jack?"

"That I cannot come to The Farm?"

"We will see. With war at hand, I must know where you are at all times. I am responsible for you. Now, bring the cart around to the shop and help me load it."

We took four loads of cedar shingles he has rived to the King's Magazine. I feel miserable that he made them while I was off with Toonahowi. At the very same time, I feel glad I saw the south end *and* the General's place.

"Shingles breathe, Little Jack. You might see stars through the Magazine roof on a clear night, but a shower will swell them tight. These here will keep the King's powder dry," Mr. Walker said proudly.

Major Harrison had soldiers unload the cart, then we went for more. After dinner, we took timbers to the fort for finishing a wall in the guard room. Soon it could be full of captured Spaniards, I thought. A chill went up my spine.

I miss Toonahowi today. He is gone. Without a word. Before dark, Mr. Walker allowed me to go over and feed the horse again. I carried water and fresh hay to his stall and I rubbed him down. He is so glossy black.

Now my arms and legs are tired. They ache.

20 June 1742

More work! Mr. Walker replaced the platform for one of the 18-pounders on the fort rampart. It had to slope to specifications.

"Mr. Walker cannot accept anything short of perfection," Major Harrison said when he inspected. That made me feel proud of Mr. Walker.

The Major lives in a good house near the Barracks. His wife, Elizabeth, is Frederica's midwife and is paid by the Trustees 5 pounds a year plus five shillings per laying. It is said that the births and burials come out about even.

Finished at the Fort, I was hoping for time to exercise and ride the horse, but Mr. Walker told me to hurry with the feeding and meet him on the way back. He had seen bees collecting on a tree at the edge of the savannah near Hurricane Plantation.

Sure enough, a swarm hung on the lowest limb of a rotten water oak there. The sound of the bees was wild and mysterious. Mr. Walker had brought a straw skep from the meadow where all of his hives were ranged in a half-circle.

We placed the skep beneath the cluster of bees. They looked like a huge bunch of grapes.

"The queen is gently disposed this day," Mr. Walker said softly. "Trim me a devil's walking stick, Little Jack."

I selected a cane, cut it with my big knife and skinned off the briars.

"Her Majesty is sendin' out her scouts to find a new home, and we have it ready right here. First, let me place

31

a chunk of honey comb at the entrance. That's their favorite food. I will sway the limb a bit with your pole ...easy...like this."

"What do you want me to do, Mr. Walker?"

"Grab that frying pan I brought along and beat it loud 'n regular...loud 'n regular."

I could not believe my eyes. Those bees - thousands of them - all golden wings and eyes in the sun - dove right into the small hole at the base of the skep!

Mr. Walker did not trust me to take the skep back to the meadow, I might trip and get stung. He carried it himself while many of the bees browsed on his face and arms without the slightest harm.

"Now, Little Jack, we have thirty-five lively skeps."

"How much honey will you get?" I asked.

"With all the gall berry bushes and fruit trees 'round here, maybe two hundred gallons if we bow low to Madam Queen." He bowed solemnly before the domed skep. I bowed too even though I felt foolish.

I shall never forget the humming of that swarm. Nor the smell and taste of a chunk of crystallized honey Mr. Walker gave me when we got home.

Bees are listed as "livestock" in the town records, but to me they are magical. They cast a spell.

21 June 1742

The sunrise was flaming over the meadow as I went to The Farm stables. I approach the horse slowly from the front and talk to him quietly. He senses my disposition. Had I known then what I now suspect, the horse might have caught my uneasiness. Because, at breakfast, Lt. Sterling, whose room is right next to mine, said that a troop of volunteers and servants was being recruited from the townsfolk. The lieutenant has instructions to commandeer horses belonging to Frederica freeholders.

This news was all over town by the time Mrs. Walker sent me to Shoemaker LeVally's who is close-mouthed as a rule, but he told me the same thing. From his shop, I ran on up Broad to the public well where notices are often posted in the well shed. Soldiers and servants meet there and gossip. A crowd had gathered, listening to a sergeant read in a loud raspy voice from a broadside.

TO KEEP UP A CHEERFUL SPIRIT
THE MAGISTRATES AND OFFICERS OF THE REGIMENT
AND OTHER INHABITANTS OF THE TOWN
ARE INVITED FOR BISCUITS AND WINE
ON THE PARADE AT THE FORT

I came back to tell the Walkers. By the time the sun was overhead, it looked as though *everyone* was headed for the Fort. You would have thought it was the Festival of St. George! The flag was displayed, General Oglethorpe himself led the toasts while guns were discharged - to His Majesty's health! To the Prince and all the Royal Family! To the honorable Trustees! To the Prosperity and Safety of This Colony! Then Capt. James Mackay, commander of the General's company, gave a final toast to Our Fearless Captain General! General Oglethorpe looked pleased and said,

"Go now to whatever tasks lie before you. This evening, a public cold Entertainment will be served at Bennett's Tavern, and those with partners may dance."

Now it is late. We have been to the Entertainment. The fiddlers have stopped. I overate ginger and sweetmeats.

In spite of all the merriment, the air is thick with apprehension. Apprehension is Mr. Walker's word. The arguments among our neighbors during the walk home continue between Mr. and Mrs. Walker downstairs. He says the Entertainment was to get our minds off impending disaster. She says the Entertainment was a sure sign that all is well.

Who is right?

22 June 1742

Toonahowi is back. Before I could ask where he had been, he said the General would need the horse immediately. We walked together to The Farm - *he* walked, I trotted to keep up.

"Little Jack, I spoke with Mr. Walker about your readying the horse at a moment's notice. He understands. But I told him little else. What I tell *you*, you must swear to keep between you and me." He turned and gave me a piercing look.

"I swear," I said. "By all that is sacred."

He walked still faster. "I am come from scouting Cumberland Island. My men reported the Spanish left St. Augustine two days ago. It is a large fleet. Over fifty ships are under sail. Yesterday, that northwest wind held the tide so high, their smaller boats made for the shelter of Cumberland Sound. With my own eyes I counted four half-galleys, two schooners, and a line of peraguas. But the guns of our schooner *Walker* anchored there, and the cannon of Fort Prince William drove them on up to the north end of Cumberland, only to find Fort St. Andrews cannon waiting. So, they are anchored in the mouth of St. Andrews Sound."

For the first time since he began talking, I felt Fear. "That is close to us, Toonahowi!"

"Yes, Little Jack, close. The General will want to ride straight down to Fort St. Simons when I tell him the numbers. Prepare the horse for him and a second for me. Not a moment is to be wasted."

Later, from the Walker's front stoop, we watched Oglethorpe's Regiment march by.

"Where you off to?" Mr. Walker called to one of the corporals he knew.

"Fort St. Simons," the soldier replied. "Say yer prayers!"

It is dark and Toonahowi is not back.

23 June 1742

Rumors are flying thicker than deer flies! The Regiment may go to Cumberland. Sailors, high up in the rigging of a ship anchored off Fort St. Simons, spotted the Spanish in St. Andrews Sound. Mrs. Walker says the General will rout them in short order. Mr. Walker does not agree, judging by the length of his prayer at dinner.

24 June 1742

Scout boats have come and gone all day at the Fort dock. There is much noise beyond the palisades. I thought of climbing that giant oak back of Dr. Hawkins' pomegranate hedge to get a look at what was going on - the way those sailors did. But sure as iron is black, the doctor's wife, Beatre, would catch me. Her wrath would make the Devil tremble. She beats her servants. And, once, when the constable went to quiet her, she broke a bottle over his head!

35

25 June 1742

Lt. Tolson docked here early this morning, and his news spread like fever. Yesterday, the General ordered three scout boats of regulars to accompany him down the Inland Passage from Jekyll to Fort St. Andrews. Tolson was in the last boat, The General in the middle one. When they started across the Sound, they were sighted by four Spanish half-galleys. Those larger boats with a stiff wind pushing them made straight for the British. The next thing Tolson saw were bursts of smoke. There was so much fire exchanged, it was impossible for him to see through the smoke, and in order to save his own men, Tolson headed his boat into the Satilla River and escaped. He is sure that Oglethorpe and the others are dead. Tolson and his men have rowed since dawn to report here to Major Heron who refused to lower the flags.

"I will not accept General Oglethorpe's loss without further confirmation," the Major said.

He has sent to Savannah for volunteers and to Darien for the Highland Independent Company of Foot.

All day I have felt a great weight upon my heart. Toonahowi was surely with the General. If they were killed, I cannot bear it.

26 June 1742

Praise be to Almighty God, Tolson's news proved to be dead wrong! Capt. Dunbar and his marines docked the schooner *Walker* down at Fort St. Simons and a runner brought word here that the General was aboard - not only

unharmed but in "high spirits". How quickly every face in this town turned to smiling.

When Toonahowi came later on, we hugged each other and laughed so loud, onlookers laughed too. He was in the General's boat all right and told me how the Spanish came about to fire on them after their first blast missed. But before the half-galleys could move into position, the two scout boats shot past and made it to Fort St. Andrews. The General commanded the garrison there to withdraw to Fort Prince William, and only this morning they saw the Spanish sail by going south.

"Separated from the main fleet, I suspected they feared many more British ships than they could engage were to follow our scout boats. Anyway, they fled, Little Jack. It was a beautiful sight!"

We laughed again. "Is the danger over, Toonahowi?"

"We can hope so," he said. "If I know The Great Man, he will not drop his guard. Not yet."

My Indian friend turned toward The Farm. "The horse will be back from the south end," he called. "He will expect you, Little Jack."

His words struck me like a blow. So much has happened the last three days, I have forgotten my duties. A good thing the horse was not here or he might have gone hungry.

27 June 1742

Mr. Walker must be mightily relieved to have the General back on St. Simons alive, because he even suggested that I spend the day with Toonahowi if I liked. But Toonahowi and General Oglethorpe are having talks with senior officers.

I rode the horse over to the Village Creek and back, then I brushed him for a long time to make up for our separation.

The rest of the day I helped Mr. Walker in the shop. His hands *know* the grain of every kind of wood. I like the smell of the shavings when I sweep them up. After all of the excitement, it felt good to be in the peace of the shop. But then Thomas Hird stopped by to ask, "Have you heard about Francis Moore?"

"Naw, what about him?" Mr. Walker said.

"The General has sent him - his own secretary - to Charles Town with one more plea for help from Governor Bull. Things must be more desperate than we are led to believe." Mr. Hird shook his head hopelessly.

How uncertain these days are. I think a lot about that and wonder what tomorrow will bring.

28 June 1742

36 ships were sighted today! The Spanish *are* coming!

29 June 1742

This afternoon, the enemy sailed up and anchored a few miles off the eastern shore of the Island. Suddenly the talk is not about whether or not we will be invaded - *when* is the question. I heard soldiers making bets. Some said two days from now, the others said a week.

Toonahowi, who comes and goes like a shadow, thinks it will depend on tides and winds. Both must be favorable for the Spanish Commanding General, Montiano, to land his troops. Thank merciful heaven there are high winds this day. Even the birds took shelter.

30 June 1742

General Oglethorpe has lost no time since getting back from Cumberland. He has sent scouts to warn every settlement in this Colony. Now English Rangers are arriving from as far away as Augusta. Indians, too. Mary Musgrove, who interpreted for the General when he first came over, sent her Creeks. Chickasaws under Squirrel King and Toonahowi's Yamacraws are already scattered throughout the woods and marshes and along the beaches here. They reconnoiter day and night.

I suspect they report directly to Toonahowi who then reports to the General. It is the wrong time to ask questions.

1 July 1742

In the middle of the night, a rooster began crowing. It wanted the sunrise to hurry as much as I did. Sleep overcame me a few times, but for most of the hours I leaned out the window to watch the coming and going from one end of Broad to the other. From the town gate to the Fort, lanterns blinked. The noise, pressed down by the moist heat, would have kept angels awake - the rattle and squeak of wagons and oxcarts, the clopping and whinneying of horses, the rumble and groan of the plank bridges over the moat, thunder flat and close. And men busily stacking ammunition, tools, equipment on the rampart. All this day, their curses, laughs, halloos still drum in my ears.

By noon, the 18-pounders commanding the river approaches were in place. The 12-pounders just south on the Point Battery are ready. Let those Spanish rapscallions come up the Frederica! Our cannon will greet them!

A warning has been posted. Drunks will be put in irons. Everyone in this town must be sober and alert. I am sober but my eyes are sticky-sleepy, my pen is sluggish.

It is raining and a high wind drowns out the hubbub. Blessed wind, drown Montiano in the Sound!

2 July 1742

When the drums beat reveille this morning for the men in the Barracks, I pretended to be one of them - washed, dressed, put my quarters in order, then went with Mr. Walker for inspection. We were lined up with other town volunteers and men servants.

For the first time, I was given a musket. It was a Brown Bess like Mr. Walker's. He had rolled a batch of cartridges which he divided with me. The Sergeant ordered us to stand six in front, six behind. With his own musket, he showed us the exercise we must learn.

Having watched the Company again and again, it was familiar to me, and when I rammed down the first cartridge, a kind of anger boiled up inside me and grew with each order.

Poise your firelock

Join your left hand to your firelock

Whole cock your firelock

Present

Fire

The explosion kicked me. Pain shot through my shoulder and neck. Instead of anger, I felt weakness - I was so weak and the gun was so heavy - my arms and legs trembled as I lowered the butt end of the musket to the ground.

Rest your firelock

Order your firelock

Powder is not plentiful and so we fired only three rounds. Once it was over, I was faint with relief. Sweat poured down my back and soaked my shirt. Mr. Walker noticed.

"Courage, John Campbell MacLeod," he said. "If duty forces us to use these arms, 'tis best we know what we are doing."

He is right, of course. But I suspect I was not the only one praying to escape so cruel a duty. All I can think about is if I must help defend this place, can I shoot another human being? I do not wish to find out.

3 July 1742

Today, bayonets are added to the drill.

"If you run out of ammunition, you will use the bayonet in fighting hand to hand," the Sergeant said in his matter-of-fact way. "Hold it rigid in front of your own body. Aim at the enemy's belly. Lunge!"

I have eaten little since. Mrs. Walker scolds, but that does not help me swallow.

4 July 1742

Mrs. Walker must not be as calm inside as she acts. To-day she has spun cotton, weeded the herb garden, scoured pewter, and picked squash! Her mouth is a tight line. She recalled that a few years ago a strange ship headed up the river. General Oglethorpe "thoroughly alarmed" everyone by acting as though an invasion was on the way. He directed some soldiers to rush into town screaming Spanish threats and firing their muskets.

"We all ran to the Fort, I can tell you," Mr. Walker said, "Every man, woman, child took up arms. Thank heaven it was a false alarm, but this time - this time it will be the real thing."

"My husband, you are a doomsayer," Mrs. Walker said. "The General will finish the Spanish once they land on the south end. Besides, the Highland Company is here. They will protect us. Isn't that right, Little Jack?"

"To hear Lt. Charles Mackay tell it," I answered.

Mackay has his men on parade every morning. Their bonnets and kilts make them look different from the Regiment who wear the red coats and cocked hats of the British Army.

It was while watching the Highlanders this morning that I felt rather than heard someone come up behind me. When I whirled around, there was Toonahowi.

"Little Jack!" He hugged me. "It seems a moon since I left you."

"It has been three days, Toonahowi, the longest days of my life." I wanted to tell him how the musket and bayonet drills took my appetite. Instead, I joked.

"Nothing has changed except my voice. Sometimes I sound very like a bull frog."

"Ah, you are growing up this summer," he laughed.

At that moment, the General rode close by us on his black horse to watch the Highlanders do their target practice at 100 yards. He gave a new broadsword to the fellow who was "best shot". Then he dismounted and talked to each unit. Toonahowi said General Oglethorpe had done the same earlier down at Fort St. Simons.

"Now that the wind has changed, Montiano will try to land the Spanish troops." Toonahowi's voice dropped to a whisper. "It is a matter of hours. But we are almost 500 strong, and we know this island - every marsh, creek, stand of woods, every open stretch of high land. The Marines know every current in the surrounding waters. Our ships *Walker, Success, Faulcon* along with a flotilla of smaller boats guard the mouth of the Frederica River. We are ready as we can be without the help of the Carolinians."

Before I could ask any questions, the General's voice rang out, "Stand by our liberties! By your King! And for this besieged Colony! May Almighty God endue you with courage and loyalty against all odds!"

Toonahowi left me to meet the General at the Barracks where they ate dinner with the officers. Later, I watched them ride out the town gate and head south on Military Road.

Since the high winds died, Frederica seems awful quiet. We are waiting...waiting...waiting....

5 July 1742

Runners from the south end began arriving with news early this morning when Montiano sent a galley and two half-galleys to sound out the channel for the Spanish fleet. They were favored by an incoming tide, a calm sea, and a favorable breeze pushing them right toward our Island.

Cannon at Fort St. Simons and the guns of our ships fired on them, but they somehow made it back to Montiano's flagship.

Every few hours the runners kept coming to Frederica until the evening drums sounded. They told what happened when Montiano weighed anchor - that was this afternoon - and his ships began firing on ours. He sank the *Faulcon*. But the *Success* and *Walker* held their own. Even so, they along with our on-shore cannon could not block the Spanish Commander. By 6 o'clock this evening, he had led his fleet northwest of Fort St. Simons near a dry marsh. Some 500 of his men were rowed in long boats to shore. Swivel-gun fire from the galleys protected them during their landing.

They must have suspected that our Indians and Rangers were hidden, spying on their every move - the woods were "watching." How can I wait to ask Toonahowi? He must have seen the enemy with his very own eyes.

6 July 1742

A bad dream waked me soon after midnight. I slipped to the window and checked the wind. Nothing stirred. The sky was thick with stars. Voices rose clearly from the dock, and I recognized them. Our scout boats were returning from the south end. What could that mean?

I could not go back to sleep but tossed and swatted palm beetles and muskettos for what seemed hours. Then I noticed a far away sound I could not place, still it was familiar. Finally, I stole to the window again. Was I awake or dreaming? A chill of fear shook me - the sound was drums. Drums. Could the Spanish have discovered the road to Frederica? Unable to move, I listened, peering into the night.

It was not until the sentry guards opened the gate that I knew for sure that it was *our* Regiment coming, it was their drums I heard. Oglethorpe's Regiment is back!

I leaned out the window and waved with both arms as they marched by, but no one noticed. Bringing up the rear were the Rangers on horseback, some of them holding soldiers in their arms - blood all over.

And last, erect and alone, there was the General on his black horse.

Retreat is the word heard over and over this day. The town is divided between those who say General Oglethorpe should have made a stand on the south end "to the last man" and those who say he is wise to combine all of his forces *here*. Mr. Walker said, "According to reports, the Spanish have so many ships and men, the Regiment, Highland Company, Indians and Rangers and Marines must not be divided."

That makes sense to me, and it is hard to hold my tongue when I hear others say things like "Oglethorpe is no military man", or "the General is foolhardy", and "giving up Fort St. Simons is the act of a coward" - on and on they wrangle.

It was Toonahowi who told me that Montiano had brought his whole army ashore during the night. Our Indians tried to make the landing difficult, and they captured five Spaniards for Oglethorpe to question.

If they told the truth, Montiano has 5,000 men. Toonahowi does not believe them. "There are not half that many," he said. Just the same, the General could not afford to have his troops on the south end overrun and cut off from Fort Frederica. So he ordered that everything down there be moved out or destroyed. All supplies, even food, were tossed into the Sound. The men drove spikes into the vents of the cannon. They cannot be fired.

The General also sent the *Success* and *Walker* up to Carolina for help and had the smaller boats burned rather than leave them to the enemy. In their rush, our soldiers left behind some livestock and weapons. Who knows what else, but Toonahowi thinks the evacuation went faster than even the General expected.

At the very same time I was watching the Regiment return, Toonahowi and his scouts were watching two companies of Montiano's grenadiers search the deserted beach and fortifications on the south end.

"By now, the whole enemy army is occupying our territory there," Toonahowi said angrily. "They will not be content to wait long. They will come for us."

His words will keep me awake again tonight. It helps that he asked me to feed and groom the General's horse first thing tomorrow morning. I need to *do* something!

7 July 1742

The sunrise was blurred by a steamy haze - a haze so layered above the meadow that I imagined Spaniards were hidden behind every tree waiting to grab me on my way to The Farm. When I entered the stable, General Oglethorpe's horse was skittish too. He stamped and snorted, impatient for me to exercise him. But we both quieted down once I began brushing his mane. I hummed and talked to him, "No horse in Georgia has sounder limbs and feet and wind, my friend." His ears cocked. "You like a bit of praise, don't you, my friend?"

"That he does!" said the General wading through clean straw toward us. "What more can a man want than a horse with a good mouth and manners, Little Jack?"

He seemed pleased with me and the horse. "Remember Shakespeare's line ..."'he trots the air, the earth sings when..., he touches it.'" The Great Man stroked and patted the horse's withers.

"This very day, he and I may be sorely tested, Little Jack. This will not be a day for ewe-necked, weedy breeds! Oh, no, he must have more fire and stamina than has the enemy. More speed. More boldness! More!"

With that he turned and hurried up the path to his cottage. I did not see him again until shortly before 10 o'clock. He was reviewing the Highland Company at drill.

Just as the Sergeant ordered, "Poise your firelocks," four Rangers, their horses slathered with sweat, charged up the street from the gate and halted before General Oglethorpe saluting.

"Sir, our patrol has exchanged fire with the Spanish!"

"Where?" the General snapped.

"Not more than a mile and a half from the town gate, Sir."

As though he had been waiting for the word, the General ordered the Regiment under Capt. Raymond Demere to assemble, and since the Highlanders were already in formation, he wheeled his horse about and commanded them to follow him.

Toonahowi and the other Indians joined the Rangers in a gallop close behind General Oglethorpe raising a big cloud of dust. I could no longer see them, but I watched the Highlanders on foot run after.

It was Toonahowi who told me what happened next. The General led them south on Military Road, then where it curves east, just this side of Gully Hole Creek, he spotted the Spanish trying to form a battle line on the opposite side of the savannah there. He directed his men to attack. The enemy, unaware of how close they were to Frederica, were so surprised, so addled by the sudden charge that they scattered their return fire in all directions. That was when Toonahowi saw one of them take square aim at him. Thank heaven, my Indian friend moved too quickly to take the enemy ball in his heart. Instead, it struck his right arm.

"He did not stop me though, Little Jack. With my flintlock pistol, I shot and killed another officer who was coming at me," Toonahowi said. "We had closed the distance between us and them too swiftly for them to get into formation. The general knew their surprise threw them off balance and took full advantage, urging the Rangers and my Indians to pursue Montiano's forward party ferociously. The Spaniards began falling back, turning and running for their lives down the road. The chase was hot for almost three miles before the General reined in his horse and ordered us to wait for the rest of the Highlanders to catch up. That gave us time to take stock of our losses in the skirmish. Only one man died, and not at the hand of the enemy. The heat overcame him. As for the Spanish, two of their captains, Sanchez and Hernandez were captured. Altogether, thirty-six of their soldiers were killed or taken prisoner by our men." Toonahowi paused, but I knew he was not altogether finished. "We were certain that Mon-

49

tiano would soon learn what had happened and would send more men up the road toward us. The General continued to move us south another couple of miles, but I could not keep up. His plan was to hide his men at the edge of a savannah bordering a narrow place in the road. The enemy will be forced to pass in single file, and our troops will be in a perfect position to hamper them." He sighed, and I knew how much he wanted to be in that action.

All of the above, Toonahowi told me while waiting his

turn at the Barracks hospital. Dr. Hawkins was busy tending first to some of the Spaniards who were about to bleed to death from bayonet gashes. The insides of one man were spilling out. I confess I looked away.

While it had been impossible to see the skirmish from the village, I did hear the crack of muskets, but I could only wonder about what was happening. And it was not until the soldiers dispatched to the site began returning with the wounded and dead that we knew for sure who had won out. When Toonahowi, barely able to walk, had staggered through the town gate, I ran to help him. He protested, "My wound is nothing." But the shock and pain in his eyes spoke the truth.

Together we had made our slow way to the hospital which was in the Barracks. Dr. Hawkins and his assistant cared for the illnesses and injuries of the King's troops there. Now, the long room was crowded with Spaniards, some twisting in agony on the floor, others propped on a bench along the wall looked scared and angry. It was the *first time* for me to be in the hospital, and it was the *first time* I put myself in the enemy soldiers' place. I was the enemy to them. They were as afraid of me as I was of them.

Dr. Hawkins talked to Toonahowi while examining his wound. He asked about the battle and the safety of General Oglethorpe. Not once did Toonahowi groan or cry out while the doctor probed with his finger for the musket ball.

"This is a simple wound, not deep," he said. "Lucky for you, you do not wear a shirt. No fibers or splinters to remove, just the ball. Here it is, clean." Dr. Hawkins laid the ball on a tray holding drugs and knives and bandages. He cleansed the wound then covered it. "This lint wrapping has been dipped in oil which will allow the wound to drain. It has already bled enough. But if it turns hot and swollen, hurry back. We will apply a poultice." Dr. Hawkins turned to me. "See that he rests, Little Jack," he said curtly and moved on to the next man who mumbled deliriously in Spanish.

A blessed relief swept over me. Toonahowi was going to be all right. Those other poor devils must stay in the hospital under guard. They were prisoners and could not so much as bury their dead before the sun set.

Toonahowi will rest in my bed. Tonight, I will sleep on the floor beside him. He admits he is too weak to go on to The Farm.

He was no more than settled here than his scouts came to report on the rest of the action this afternoon. He listened carefully to every word they said. After setting up the ambush on the narrowest point in the road just this side of the southern marsh, General Oglethorpe left Demere's Company to defend the eastern edge of the road, the Rangers and Highlanders on the western side. They waited, hidden by piled up logs and brush and behind the trees of the woods close on three sides, while the General rode pell mell back to Frederica. Here, he assembled the rest of the Scouts and Rangers, Carr's Marine Company, and the Regiment. At about 3 o'clock this afternoon, he ordered them to follow him down Military Road. When they were a short distance from the ambush, they were shocked to meet Capt. Demere with three platoons of his regulars retreating from the steady, overwhelming fire being returned by a Spanish column led by Capt. Antonio Barba. They had fallen into the British trap but were fighting "with great spirit".

According to Demere, a light rain fell suddenly over the scene of battle, making the smoke too thick to see his troops, and he figured they had little choice but to give up and escape into the woods. The General, who could plainly hear continuous bursts of musket fire, refused to believe all was lost and ordered the fleeing platoons to turn around and follow him into battle.

When he reached the site of ambush, he found the rest of Demere's men still holding the eastern position under Lt. Sutherland and Sgt. Stewart. On the west, Lt. Charles Mackay's Highlanders, with the Rangers, remained firmly in command, and they kept firing even as the Spanish began withdrawing. Capt. Barba was already marching his grenadiers and regulars - there may have been 300 of them - back towards Fort St. Simons. His ammunition was running low, and he knew he was in danger of being surrounded and outnumbered by the British.

I can imagine how surprised and relieved the General was by that sight! The main battle had been fought without him, decided by Sutherland's and Mackay's brave men who refused to give one inch. They were the ones outnumbered! But the enemy never caught on!

Toonahowi questioned his scouts over and over as though the news was too good for him to believe, but when they convinced him they had told him the facts just as they had happened, he let out a whoop of joy. The scouts and I joined in, and the Walkers laughed at us with relief.

After the scouts left, everyone went on discussing this day of quirky fighting and the aloofness of Montiano who failed to take personal command of his forces. Toonahowi says that was because Montiano underestimated British resolve and tactics. He was unprepared for battle in this island's tangle of woods and marshes with the fiercest Indians and Scots and Regulars ever assembled.

The General's soldiers are with him tonight somewhere south of here on Military Road. They will camp as near as they dare to Fort St. Simons while the Indians scout the Spanish defenses. We expect they will regroup. Toonahowi says he will be back in action tomorrow.

Tomorrow there will be more burials.

8 July 1742

Around noon today, General Oglethorpe led his troops back to Fort Frederica after his scouts reported that the Spanish were sticking close to the south end fortifications. And, finally, Capt. Horton's company with the Fort St. Andrews garrison landed from Cumberland soon after. The important thing is they crossed the Sound unchallenged by the Spanish. Could this mean Montiano has given up? I cannot wait to ask Toonahowi.

Everyone here figures the enemy will next sail up the river and assault Fort Frederica. The soldiers have been put to work improving our defenses. The townsfolk are assigned jobs, too. I must help Mr. Walker replace rotten boards in the deck where the fort cannon recoil. We hear

Oglethorpe's men arguing over how many Spaniards have been killed.

"I say around 200," one corporal bragged.

"Naw, you better cut that in two," another said.

"Half of *that*," said a third man. "50 bodies would be my guess, not countin' those 8 our scouts ambushed today sneakin' up here."

One thing is for sure, the sight of dead and wounded grenadiers strewn through the marshes is bound to have frayed the Spaniards' nerve.

"Their morale has sunk as low as a rattle snake's belly," the corporal said. "One of our spies reported as much to my Officer."

By now, our ships have arrived in Charles Town. They will be back any day with reinforcements. Montiano knows that. He knows, too, that if he does not get his army and fleet out of here in order, the governor of Cuba will have him hanged!

9 July 1742

Capt. Hernandez escaped from his guards today. Believe me, that caused excitement. The guards face a court martial once this bigger trouble is settled. After all Hernandez can give Montiano a true account of the Gully Hole Creek battle as well as an idea of the limited number of men here. Montiano may not know how many cannon are within the Fort, but he now knows of its unfinished condition. This military post is on full alert.

In spite of that, the soldiers must take time to dig graves. Mr. Walker and I have become exhausted, building buryin' boxes and nailing down the lids.

"Enough to make you puke, this stench of dried blood and spoilin' flesh," Mr. Walker said. "On such a sultry hot day, the rotten smell from Frederica's privies is like the scent of lemons by comparison."

He sounded gruff, but he and Mrs. Walker are sad as am I. I shall always smell and see and feel the horror of this burial place outside the town gate.

10 July 1742,

Toonahowi was strong enough to walk with me to the Fort today. He is still disappointed because he missed the action yesterday when some of his Indians killed a boatload of the Spanish in search of drinking water. Montiano's supply is low. If he stays on, he must have water for his troops. General Oglethorpe and Toonahowi were talking about that when scouts - all out of breath - ran up from the Point Battery.

"General, we have sighted 3 enemy boats - a galley with 2 half-galleys - rounding the bend down the river there." They pointed and gestured. "The enemy boats are headed this way!"

Just as General Oglethorpe had expected, Montiano was sending a party to fathom the waters off Fort Frederica. The Spanish leader would attack the Fort then land his troops along the river bank. But the General was far ahead of him. His 18-pounders and howitzers were waiting for this very moment. He had only to give the order and the whole river exploded! Blasts of fire and smoke deafened and blinded me. *Boom Boom Boom* the great cannon balls zoomed over the water, and other projectiles arched higher, and plumes of water shot up into the summer air where the balls landed in the river.

When the bombardment ended and the smoke drifted on and on across the marsh opposite, the rowers of the Spanish galleys had turned and sped back down the Frederica River. The General with Toonahowi and scouts leaped into their boats and gave chase all the way past the bend. Again, the Spanish fled!

11 July 1742

One of our seamen who was taken prisoner back in May, escaped from the Spanish fleet and made his way here. I have not met him. His name is Samuel Cloake. His report on the enemy is being discussed up and down Broad Street. He claims the Spanish fighters are now "downhearted." He tells how scared they are of our cannon and our Indians, and how the Cuban troops are urging Montiano to sail back to St. Augustine while the weather is good - his first duty after all *is* to protect Florida and Havana. But the Floridians urge Montiano to press the invasion here and get revenge for their losses.

"Oglethorpe should take advantage of this quarrel," Toonahowi says. "He can make up Montiano's mind for him!" My Indian friend and his "Great Man" are some pair.

"I must spend the night at The Farm, Little Jack," Toonahowi said, as he left me at the town gate. "The General and I may talk all night planning the next move."

Ever since he stayed here, this room seems empty without him.

12 July 1742

While at The Farm grooming the black horse this morning, I saw Lt. Charles Mackay and Capt. Mark Carr ride up. Toonahowi met them at the front door of the General's cottage. I had been back here for three hours before they returned to the Fort. Some pow-wow!

My curiosity is running away with me. Mrs. Walker watched me at supper like a hawk, because my hominy bowl "emptied only once". The talk around our table was the same as in every house in Frederica - what would Montiano do now? The question which plagues me even more is what is General Oglethorpe up to?

Late this evening, he and his officers marched with their men through the gate down Military Road again - the Highlanders, Carr's Marines, a couple of troops of Rangers, and at least half of the Regiment. The General is up to something, that's for sure.

13 July 1742

It turns out that the British planned to slip up and terrorize the Spanish camp last night. But a mysterious thing happened. The musket of one of Carr's men blasted off in the stillness - a dead give away. He said it was an accident, but he was a Frenchman - a spy probably - because he ran away toward the Spanish lines.

His surprise spoiled, General Oglethorpe began sending his troops back up to the Fort rather than risk a battle on Military Road again. First, though, he ordered the drummers to spread out through the woods and "beat the Grenadiers march". They kept that up for half an hour which must have made it seem the General had more men than he really did.

"That has been his tactic right along," Toonahowi said. And laughed. "The bombardment from the Fort's cannon three days ago was plotted and timed to make our fortifications seem far more powerful than they are."

Then Toonahowi told me about a letter the General wrote this morning to the Frenchman who is bound to have told Montiano all he knows. A Spanish prisoner was released to deliver the letter. It was written as though the Frenchman were *our* spy, and in the letter he was told to give Montiano a *low* count of British forces. The letter also told the Frenchman to offer to guide the Spanish fleet up the Frederica River into the waiting arms of the British before the Carolinian ships, expected at any moment, arrived.

Of course, the letter never reached the Frenchman. Just as Oglethorpe had hoped, it was taken straight to Montiano.

Shortly after noon, Toonahowi's scouts brought word that 5 British ships were sighted off the coast. Montiano must be mighty confused! Could the Carolinians be sending help? "That is a miracle the General no longer counted on," Toonahowi said. "But Montiano does not know that. He is bound to wonder if a whole fleet approaches this Island."

"If so, he could be trapped here," I said gleefully. "He could be trapped by the British navy in front of him and by our soldier's closing in from the north."

I doubt that Montiano will sleep much tonight. I know I will not.

14 July 1742

No sooner had I blown out my candle last night than I fell fast asleep. It was a surprise to wake rested. Instead of my usual nightmares, I had a beautiful dream. I dreamed that the Spanish were sailing out across the Sound, one tall sail after another and another and another fading over the horizon like ghosts.

It seemed so real I almost told it at breakfast, but Mr. Walker would think me foolish. "Put no stock in dreams," he would say.

Imagine how odd I felt when we learned a bit later that during the night, the great bold Spanish commander, Montiano, had begun breaking camp - destroying Fort St. Simons - loading equipment and men on his numerous boats in full retreat! Toonahowi's scouts are watching the withdrawal, and runners bring reports here in relays. They report that the large ships have gone by sea.

My dream has come true. I will tell Toonahowi.

Half-galleys and smaller boats are still being loaded with supplies and soldiers. One is said to carry old Montiano himself. They are headed down the inland waterway.

Around the public well where a soldier kept posting the latest word, it seemed everyone in this town crowded together. Neighbors who had not spoken for a year, shook hands in greeting. Rivals, such as Magistrate Calwell and Dr. Hawkins, acted glad to stand side by side. Even Mrs. Hawkins was both happy and sober, if you know what I mean. Some of the ladies cried for joy. I thought Constable Hird was going to preach us a thanksgiving sermon when he opened his big Prayer Book, but all he managed to say was, "The infidel has given up at last! The Spanish have given up! The Almighty has delivered us from the hands of our mortal enemy! Let us pray." Then he bowed his head, but no words came, and for a moment there was a kind of holy silence before the crowd began chattering again, and the children darted about playing tag.

When the Regiment and Highland Company formed on parade at 10 o'clock, the crowd cheered, drowning out the bagpipes and drums. They hoped for General Oglethorpe. I imagine he will come tomorrow and bestow special honors and promotions.

At dinner, Mr. Walker said something I liked, "It is as though our town is taking a deep breath - as though a sweet

60

wind of relief has pushed away the clouds of conflict which threatened us."

Afterward, he walked with me back to the public well. He stayed there in the crowd talking, but I wandered down toward the dock near the Fort's southwest bastion, wishing for the sight of Toonahowi.

Sure enough, his scouts had just brought him from the Bluff on the southern branch of the river. With one leap, he was out of the boat onto the dock beside me. For an instant we looked at one another, then his arms were around me in a bear hug. "I have seen for myself the Spanish on their way to St. Augustine, Little Jack," he said. "After all these days and nights of extreme anxiety and constant danger, it is almost too much to believe that they have at last given up."

It was the right moment to tell him my dream of the enemy ships sailing away. "That was a good sign, Little Jack," he said. "The Great Man has secured this colony for the Crown. Far more than I have dared tell you, Frederica has lived on the very edge of destruction, but you people here did not panic as some on the mainland did. Nor did our forces despair. I am sure the General will soon declare a day of celebration, and he will praise the valor of his men and of the inhabitants of this island stronghold."

What a day for speeches, I thought. There was much I wanted to say to him, but a great lump in my throat stopped me. I did manage to ask, "How many did we lose in battle?"

"I do not know yet. Fewer than ten probably - fewer than a fourth of the Spanish dead. They do not know how to fight from behind trees. Besides, they are poor shots. I am proof of that!"

"Thank God you are healed of your wound."

"Yes, we owe much to Providence, Little Jack."

I saw tears fill his eyes and I no longer tried to hide my own. Toonahowi must have known, because he said, "Only strong men are not ashamed of their deep feelings."

He untied a pouch he carried at his waist, reached inside and held out a small package.

"General Oglethorpe, who has, like me, become fond of you, Little Jack, asked me to give you these silver buttons from the uniform he wore into battle a week ago. They are not only beautiful, they will remind you for all the days of your life of the summer of 1742 when you served a great man well."

I could not speak. Toonahowi put his arm about my shoulder. We stood there, quiet in the sunlight, looking at our flag bright against the blue sky over Fort Frederica's ramparts.

It meant more than ever before that it was still there.